The Baby Book

Written and illustrated by
Kathy Cruickshank

A GOLDEN BOOK • NEW YORK
Western Publishing Company, Inc., Racine, Wisconsin 53404

There are so many babies.
There are big babies. There are
small babies.

There are quiet babies…

and loud babies.

There are babies with brown eyes…

and babies with blue eyes.

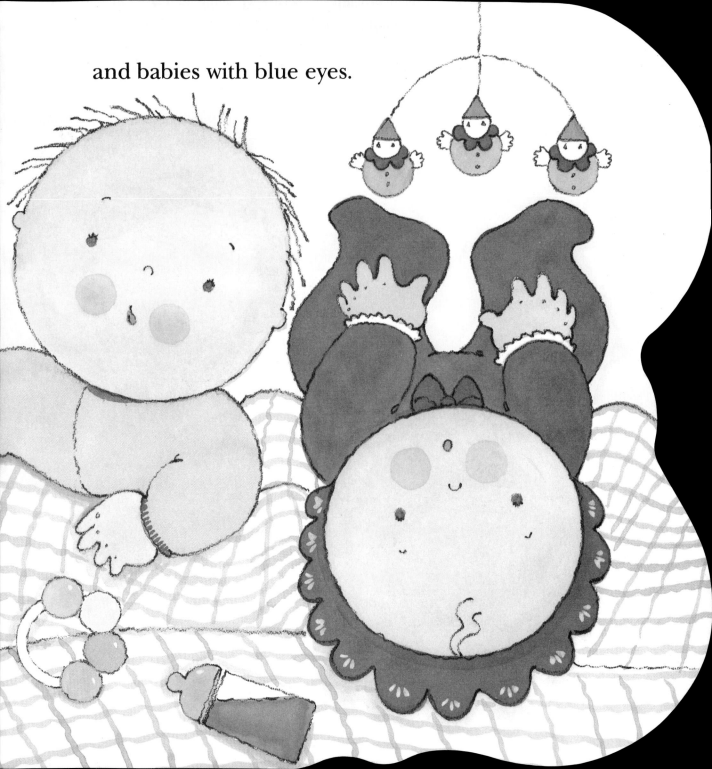

Some babies have no hair.

Some babies have lots of hair.

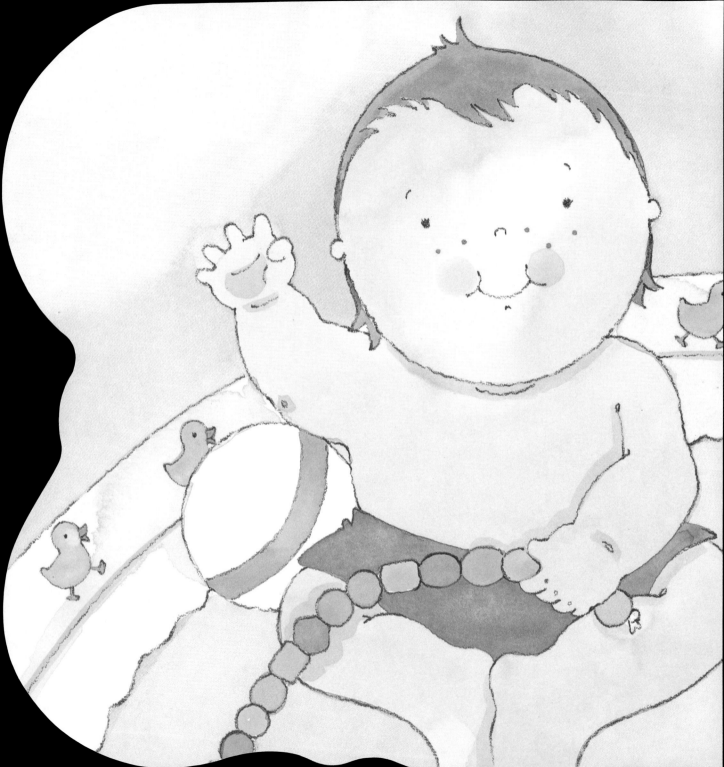

Some babies look alike.
They are called twins.
Can you tell
who is who?

All babies like to be held.
Cuddling a baby is nice.

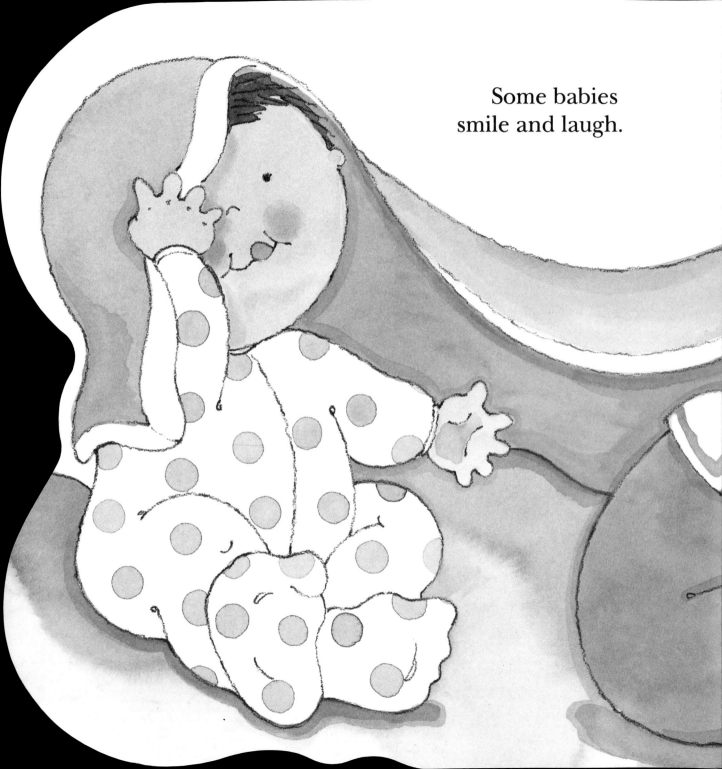

Some babies
smile and laugh.

They make
silly faces.

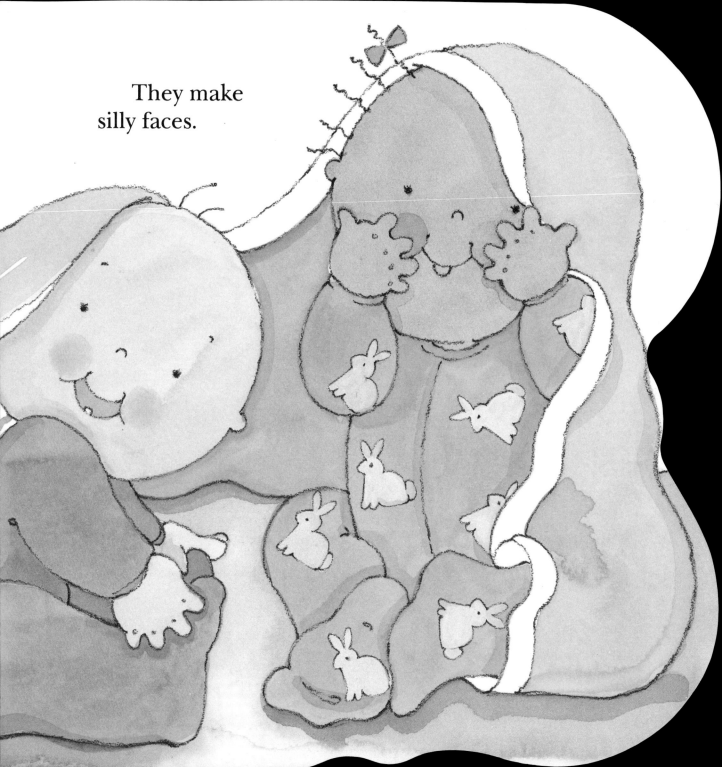

Babies like to eat.
At first they need
help. But soon
babies can eat
by themselves.

Babies are very curious. They like playing with new things.

Going shopping is fun. At the store, babies have lots to look at, touch, and smell.

Playing in the park is fun, too.
Babies can swing way up high,
or they can ride play horses
that bounce.

Soon all babies grow up.
They get bigger and bigger—
just like you!